Bantam Books in the Choose Your Own Adventure® series
Ask your bookseller for the books you have missed

MASTER OF JUDO

BY RICHARD BRIGHTFIELD

ILLUSTRATED BY FRANK BOLLE

An Edward Packard Book

A BANTAM SKYLARK BOOK®
NEW YORK • TORONTO • LONDON • SYDNEY • AUCKLAND

RL4, age 10 and up

MASTER OF JUDO

A Bantam Book/June 1994

CHOOSE YOUR OWN ADVENTURE® is a registered
trademark of Bantam Books,
a division of Bantam Doubleday Dell Publishing Group, Inc.
Registered in U.S. Patent and Trademark Office and elsewhere.

Original conception of Edward Packard

Cover art by Bill Schmidt
Interior illustrations by Frank Bolle

ISBN 0-553-56397-1

Published simultaneously in the United States and Canada

Bantam Books are published by Bantam Books, a division of
Bantam Doubleday Dell Publishing Group, Inc. Its trademark,
consisting of the words "Bantam Books" and the portrayal of a
rooster, is Registered in U.S. Patent and Trademark Office and
in other countries. Marca Registrada. Bantam Books, 1540
Broadway, New York, New York 10036.

PRINTED IN THE UNITED STATES OF AMERICA

OPM   0 9 8 7 6 5

For Bill Kispert

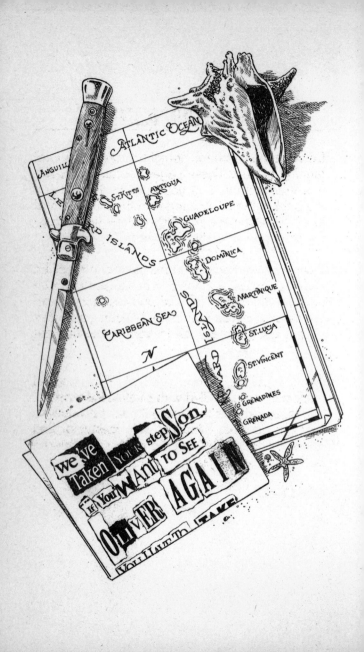

WARNING!!!

Do not read this book straight through from beginning to end. These pages contain many different adventures that you may have when you are offered the chance to teach the martial art of judo to the stepson of a billionaire—while cruising through the exotic Caribbean Sea.

From time to time as you read along, you will be asked to make a choice. The adventures you have are the results of your choices. You are responsible because you choose. After you make your decision, follow the instructions to find out what happens to you next.

Think carefully before you act. The tropical lands you visit are filled with pirates, kidnappers, and other dangers that will put your judo skills to the test. You may remain a judo master or find yourself adrift and alone, bound for the bottom of the sea.

Good luck!

You are an honor student in your school and also a black belt in the martial art of judo. It's one week before summer vacation, but you haven't even thought about taking things easy. You have final exams to take, a judo tournament to prepare for, and a summer job to find. You jump out of bed ready for a busy day.

After you get dressed, you throw your judo gear and schoolbooks into your knapsack and hurry downstairs to breakfast. Your mother, father, and younger sister are already sitting at the kitchen table.

"How's your search for a summer job coming?" your father asks.

"No luck yet," you say. "I guess I should have started looking weeks ago."

"How about a job at the movie theater?" your sister suggests. "It's pretty busy in the summer."

"Not a bad idea, sis," you say, glancing at the clock. You've got about thirty seconds if you want to catch the school bus. You take a last bite of toast, grab your knapsack, and rush out the door.

Turn to page 2.

2

After school, you stop by the movie theater on your way to judo practice. Mr. Pierce, the theater owner and manager, is in the ticket booth getting things ready for the first showing. You ask him about a job.

"Sorry," he says. "I'm automating everything. A vending machine will sell the tickets, and a computer will control the projection. I can sit home and keep track of things on a TV monitor."

"Well, thanks anyway," you say, trying to hide your disappointment. You walk on to the Martial Arts Center, wondering if you'll ever be able to find a job.

When you arrive, you change into your *judogi,* a loose white cotton jacket and pants, and your black belt. You bow to your *sensei,* or teacher, Mr. Yamamoto, as you enter the practice hall of the dojo. Then you kneel for your preliminary meditation. These thought and breathing exercises help you to focus your mind and increase your concentration. After that, you are ready to begin your warm-up.

Go on to the next page.

All around you, other class members do the same. Everyone is preparing for the tournament, which will include competitors from throughout the state.

"Today we review some of our *wazas,* or attacking movements," Mr. Yamamoto announces a short time later. "We will then combine them into *katas,* or attacking routines."

The *sensei* calls on you and your friend, Chuck Nelson, to demonstrate.

Turn to page 4.

You and Chuck walk to the center of the hall and bow first to Mr. Yamamoto, then to the assembled group, and then to each other.

With a quick but easy movement, you grab the fabric at Chuck's arm with both your hands. At the same time, you slip your foot behind him. You lean down and forward—and yank.

Chuck goes flying over your back, landing with a thump on the thick mat that covers the floor of the practice hall. He gets up, and the two of you bow to each other again. Then he demonstrates the same throw on you. Chuck throws you even higher than you threw him.

You pick yourself up, smiling. Chuck can't help smiling too. Mr. Yamamoto gives you both a stern look. You and Chuck bow to each other again, this time with serious expressions on your faces.

Turn to page 16.

6

"We're going to pay a visit to some friends of Robbie's up in the mountains," Julius says cooly. "He's waiting there with Oliver. I'm throwing the three of you in as a bonus."

"You kidnapped Oliver and are holding him for ransom?" you ask.

"No, not ransom," Julius says. "We're getting paid by Zorkin to keep him out of the way permanently."

"You rat. You planned this whole thing," Leila says.

"More or less," Julius says. "Robbie and I wanted to grab Oliver in the craft market. But Port Royal worked out just as well. It's one of Robbie's hideouts."

The cab has slowed down and is now creeping up the mountain. "Faster!" Julius shouts, waving his gun.

"I can go no fasta," the driver says. "Very steep climb."

Turn to page 17.

"I see that you have studied Oriental philosophy," Soto says to you.

"Some," you reply modestly.

"What next, then?" Oliver asks.

You demonstrate a series of warm-up exercises and a few basic moves. Then you have Oliver try them out. He is a fast learner and does them well.

After a while you tell Oliver to take a rest. "That's enough for today," you say. "We'll have another lesson tomorrow."

"I think we will reach Jamaica tomorrow," Soto says.

"Then whenever we can," you answer.

Turn to page 76.

8

You wait on deck, staring out at the ocean. A low-lying island slowly comes into view. Soon the *Alcor* enters a broad bay and drops anchor across from a picturesque town on the shore. A large cruise ship is also anchored nearby.

A hulking man with a blond crew cut rows you ashore in a lifeboat. He leaves you alone at the end of a pier and heads back to the ship. For a moment you stand there in a panic, wondering if you've done the right thing.

"May I be of assistance?" A friendly voice comes from behind you.

You turn to see a constable immaculately dressed in a white uniform.

"Yes," you say. "I've been—"

"Put ashore by Captain Hardy of the *Alcor*," he says, finishing the sentence for you.

"How did you know that?" you ask.

"I would recognize the *Alcor* anywhere. And Captain Hardy, he is well-known in the Bahamas—notorious, one might say. As you can see, his ship is already leaving," the constable says, pointing. "A wise move, otherwise I'd be tempted to send a patrol boat to him and ask some difficult questions. He has accumulated many sizable gambling debts in the islands."

"All I want to do is get back to the United States," you say.

Turn to page 72.

"This be our beach," one of them says. "We charge for passin' here."

"How much do you charge?" you ask.

"That be dependin' on how much you have," another one says. You notice that he is carrying a large knife.

A slight motion of Soto's head signals you that the other two men are coming up behind you—fast.

You and Soto pretend not to notice until they are almost on top of you. With split-second timing, you each dodge sideways. Then, using a basic judo technique, you grab one attacker and swing him full force into one of the men in front of you. There is a crack as their skulls collide. They stagger off, dazed and holding their heads.

Turn to page 96.

With a burst of adrenaline, you lunge for the rope. You grab hold of it. At the same moment, Oliver surfaces next to you, struggling to stay afloat. You hold on to the rope with one hand and grab Oliver with the other. Fortunately, Tom has let go.

The helicopter pulls you and Oliver along the surface at the end of the rope until you are well away from the lifeboat and the overturned raft. Then it descends to a few feet above the ocean. You manage to pull yourself up onto one of the runners of the helicopter and then squeeze into the small cabin. Then you pull Oliver aboard.

"My name is Mike," the pilot shouts over the sound of the motor. "Put on your safety belts, I'm heading for shore."

The helicopter rises a few hundred feet into the air and heads east. You look back and see the *Alcor* and the submarine, now miniature vessels in the distance.

The helicopter is buzzing toward shore when, twenty minutes later, the motor begins to cough. It doesn't sound good.

"Is anything the matter?" you ask.

"Just a little matter of my oil gauge dropping fast. Must be an oil leak," Mike says.

"What does that mean?" you say.

"It means we're going to have to ditch in the ocean," Mike says, his voice amazingly cool. "Don't worry. I've got a life raft with an automatic radio rescue beacon."

Turn to page 33.

"Wow!" Oliver exclaims. "Henry Morgan! He was a very famous pirate, wasn't he?"

"A kind of pirate, the greatest privateer of them all," Leila says. "He attacked the Spanish treasure ships and plundered the richest settlement in the New World, Panama City. It's said that he buried a huge treasure stolen from that city somewhere on the long stretch of sand you just rode over."

"What happened to the city of Port Royal?" you ask. "I don't see much here now."

"It was suddenly wiped from the face of the earth—in the year 1692," Leila says. "Some say it was the wrath of God that destroyed it. In any event, an earthquake and a great tidal wave swept it into the sea."

"That's quite a story," you say.

"Yes. Well, I'll tell you more once I get some food—and some water. My throat is parched," Leila says.

"That looks like a café of some kind over there," you say, pointing to a tin shack down the beach. "At least there are a few tables and chairs outside."

Go on to the next page.

"I believe it is," Leila says. "Let's give it a try."

"I want to hunt for treasure—Henry Morgan's treasure," Oliver says.

"People be lookin' for that for many years," Robbie says, "and never found it. But I know where we might find a piece of eight."

"A piece of eight?" Oliver asks.

"That's an old Spanish coin," Leila says.

Turn to page 42.

14

You follow Julius to a large cabin. Most of the crew is sitting at a table anchored to the floor.

Leila stands up and introduces you to the group. "You already know Captain Hardy, Soto, and Julius," she says. "And this is Tom, our ship's engineer and general maintenance man." He nods to you as he is introduced.

"Sean O'Brien, our first mate, is on duty. You'll meet him later." Leila goes on. "This is Ari, our chef," she says, pointing to a boy not much older than you who has just entered from the galley. "And here is your pupil, Oliver."

Oliver looks about eight or nine years old. He is thin, with a full head of uncombed dark hair.

You hold out your hand for Oliver to shake, but he ignores it, folding his arms over his chest. "I don't want a baby-sitter," he says.

"I'm your judo instructor, not a baby-sitter," you answer.

"I don't want a judo instructor either," Oliver says. "I want someone to teach me how to use a gun. You know, like they do on television—*pow! pow! pow!*" Oliver spins around, pretending to shoot everybody with his finger.

"A gun is not going to do you any good if somebody gets the drop on you first," Julius says.

"That's right," you say. "You need to be able to protect yourself no matter what the situation. Judo, if learned properly, is a form of self-defense that can help you do that."

Turn to page 62.

16

After the practice session, you and Chuck go out into the hallway and sit on a long bench while you put on your shoes.

"I'm going to start a business this summer cutting lawns," Chuck says. "Maybe you'd be interested in going in on it with me."

"Sounds good," you say. "I haven't been able to find anything else."

As you and Chuck start making plans, you see the door at the other end of the hallway open. The director of the center, Jonathan Ross, comes out and heads your way. He is a large man and a master of all the martial arts.

"I'd like to speak to you in my office," Ross tells you in a sharp tone.

You wonder for a moment if you have broken any of the rules of the center. Chuck waves good-bye with a worried look.

Turn to page 52.

The cab reaches the top of a rise. On the other side, the road drops sharply. The cab picks up speed rapidly as it goes down. The driver seems to be losing control.

"Okay," Julius says. "Now you're going too fast. Slow down."

"I canna do it, mon! Me brakes are no good!"

"Don't give me that," Julius says. "You're trying to—"

Your scream drowns out Julius's voice, and you clutch the seat in front of you. There's a hairpin turn ahead, and the cab is still accelerating. A moment later, you fly off the road at sixty miles an hour, airborne but plummeting quickly from a fifty-foot-high cliff.

The End

18

You tell the captain about what you think you saw.

"A periscope! I'm not surprised," he says. "I've had a feeling all along that we were being followed."

"But who would—"

"Pirates. Modern-day pirates," he interrupts. "My guess is that they'd like to kidnap Oliver and hold him for a huge ransom from his billionaire stepfather. But they won't get away with it. I have armament—even depth charges—aboard."

"You mean you expect a submarine attack?" you say.

He ignores your question. "It's time to turn the *Alcor* into a warship," he says.

Within the hour, the captain calls an emergency meeting of everyone in the dining room. "We have heavy-caliber machine guns fore and aft," he announces. "They need to be uncovered and made operational. We also have a cannon mounted on the bow. I'm assigning everyone to a battle station."

"Captain," Leila says, "do you really think that—"

Go on to the next page.

"I don't think, I know," the captain bellows. "We must be on guard. No lights at night. We run fast and silent."

The captain drops one of his depth charges astern, causing an undersea boom and a geyser of water. "Maybe that will scare them off," he says.

You don't know if it did, but at least no attacking submarine ever appears.

Turn to page 27.

20

When you tell Oliver you won't go, he throws a tantrum. The others try to reason with him.

Another shot lands in the ocean, this time very close to the ship. The *Alcor* rocks violently from the blast.

"The next shot will hit your ship below the waterline," the man with the megaphone says. "We are losing patience. You have thirty seconds."

"Oliver," Leila says, "you'll have to go. Otherwise we'll all die—and then there's no way we can protect you. I don't think they intend to hurt you."

Oliver nods and blows his nose. "Okay," he says.

"Are you all crazy!" O'Brien, the first mate, shouts as he rushes over. "Can't you see that they're just modern-day pirates?"

Soto steps in front of him. "Oliver will be all right. Get the lifeboat ready," Soto tells you.

You and Soto get Oliver into the lifeboat and start to row him across to the sub. O'Brien is still fuming on the deck of the *Alcor*. You wonder why O'Brien is suddenly so interested in Oliver's safety.

You are about midway to the sub when you look back and see O'Brien and Tom, the ship's engineer, in a small rubber raft paddling furiously after you. You and Soto begin rowing faster, but the lifeboat is not designed for speed. O'Brien's raft soon catches up.

Turn to page 38.

You decide to fight Chuck. You wonder if he is as concerned about the match as you are, but you don't get a chance to talk to him before the finals.

You and Chuck bow to each other across the mat. Then the match begins. As soon as you approach him, you realize that Chuck isn't fully concentrating. Also, you have practiced together so many times that you each know the other's moves perfectly.

You circle each other. Every time one of you positions yourself for an attack, the other automatically blocks the move. This goes on until the end of the time period. Ross calls *hantei,* which means that the two judges will have to decide the winner. You and Chuck bow to each other and leave the mat.

Though you didn't execute any spectacular moves, one of the judges decides in your favor. The other judge gives the decision to Chuck. It's now up to Ross, as the referee, to break the tie and decide the winner.

There is a hushed silence in the hall as Ross looks at you and then at Chuck. Finally he points at Chuck. There is quiet and polite applause from the audience.

You are relieved that Chuck has won the tournament. But you wonder if Ross really gave the decision to Chuck because you backed out of the *Alcor* assignment. You'll never know.

The End

The following days are calm and peaceful as you cruise through the crystal blue water. You give Oliver a judo lesson every afternoon. Soto also joins in. You start by teaching Oliver how to fall properly.

"Much of judo practice is spent throwing someone or being thrown," you say. "You have to overcome the fear of being thrown before you can work on your attack."

"Aren't you supposed to *keep* from being thrown?" Oliver asks.

"Not necessarily," you say. "If you fall correctly and come out of it properly, you may actually be in a better attack position."

"How do I fall, then?" Oliver asks.

"First," you say, "tuck in your chin to prevent your head from whiplashing on the mat. Then, if possible, let your right shoulder blade take the fall. And, very importantly, don't reach out for the mat with your hands. Your hands or your arms can be damaged if they get caught under your falling body."

"Wow!" Oliver exclaims. "That sounds hard."

"No, not really," you say. "We'll start off from a crouched position. Just roll backward and get the feel of it. When you have that under control, we'll practice 'breakfalls'—forward rolls like the ones they do in gymnastics."

Oliver proves to be a good student. After a few days he begins to understand the basics of judo.

Turn to page 59.

You decide to look around the ship.

You walk quietly down the companionway past the door of your cabin. You listen for a minute to make sure no one is around, then you continue to the back of the ship. There, a ladder leads to an upper level of cabins.

You climb up carefully and come out in another corridor. You creep along toward the captain's quarters, then stop to listen again. Muffled voices float through the door of one of the cabins. You can't really hear the conversation, but you can make out a few phrases such as "when we get rid of Oliver," "overboard," and "big payoff."

"Hear anything interesting?" a voice from behind you says, making you jump.

You turn to see Julius standing there. He has a gun in his hand, and it's pointed at you.

"I was just looking for my cabin, and I got the corridors mixed up," you say.

"Maybe yes, maybe no," Julius sneers. "Let's ask the captain his opinion."

Julius knocks on the cabin door. It opens, and the captain's face appears. "Yes, what is it?" he asks.

"Guess who I caught listening outside your door?" Julius says.

"Our judo instructor!" the captain says. "How much did you hear?"

Turn to page 37.

26

"I'll radio to Zorkin," the captain says. "No doubt he'll send a lawyer to handle the case. The Jamaican authorities could keep the *Alcor* tied up in port indefinitely. You and the others are material witnesses. Better to get out of here fast and clear up any legal misunderstandings later."

You and Leila begin to argue but realize that it's no use. The captain has made up his mind.

"I'm setting our course due east," Captain Hardy says. "We'll drop anchor at Charlotte Amalie on St. Thomas in the Virgin Islands."

Turn to page 67.

The next morning, when you step out on deck, Leila is leaning against the railing, holding binoculars to her eyes. You see an island rising up out of the sea ahead of you.

"That's Martinique," she says as you move next to her. "It's as French as Paris. It is, in fact, a department of France and sends delegates to the French parliament. It has also known tragedy. In 1902, Mt. Pelée, a volcano at the north end of the island, erupted and in a matter of minutes wiped out the beautiful city of St. Pierre and all its inhabitants. The explosion was so tremendous that some of the debris fell on Jamaica, eleven hundred miles away."

"That's amazing," you say. You also think that Leila herself is amazing. She seems to know everything.

The *Alcor* docks in Fort-de-France, the capital and main harbor of the island. Captain Hardy goes ashore briefly to talk to the customs officials.

"What luck," he says when he returns. "The island is in the middle of a festival."

You can see from the yacht that the streets along the waterfront are packed with costumed dancers. The air is filled with the constant throbbing of drums.

Turn to page 40.

"It seems that they've had a falling out of late," Banon says. "Your stepfather has had some severe financial difficulties and is eager to get his hands on your inheritance. We have evidence that he intended to have you killed."

You let out a breath. "What does Oliver do now?" you ask. "He can't go home."

"The Eagle has arranged for his schooling at one of the better academies in the islands. I'm not at liberty to say which one."

"Will you go there with me and still be my judo teacher?" Oliver asks.

"Sure, kid," you say. "That's part of my summer job."

The End

You have one match to go before you will fight Chuck. You know what to do. Your opponent is Jimmy Harper, a good fighter—not as good as you, but almost.

You face Jimmy across the mat at the beginning of the match and bow. Ross, the referee, calls out *hajime,* indicating you are to begin.

Jimmy starts toward you. You pretend to go for a leg sweep against his right foot. Jimmy pulls back his right leg in defense. Instead of following through with the sweep, you plant your foot firmly on the ground and grab him around the waist. Then you turn your body, twisting him off balance. He falls to the mat.

A round of applause goes up as the judges award you seven points for the throw. This is almost enough to win the match.

Turn to page 69.

You cut through a small break in the parade and race around the crowd. Soto is right behind you.

When you reach the other side of the street, you double back toward where you last saw Oliver. You spot him, still being carried by the skeleton, a hundred yards ahead. A second later, the skeleton ducks through a gateway.

You and Soto follow. As you reach the gateway, several more red devils jump out and block your path. One of them, armed with a knife, charges directly at you. You grab his wrist with your left hand and his elbow with your right, then twist sharply. The knife flies out of his hand. It goes clattering across the cobblestone street.

At the same time, Soto stops one attacker with a forward kick and another with a backward kick, the two blows in quick succession.

You and Soto race through the gateway into a small courtyard. The skeleton sets Oliver down, keeping a choke hold on his neck while he works to open an inside gate. Oliver remembers what you've taught him. He kicks hard to the rear with his heel, catching the skeleton in the ankle. The skeleton lets out a yelp as Oliver breaks loose.

The skeleton tries to escape through the gate. But he is in pain and has trouble with the latch. You and Soto grab him and pull off his mask.

Turn to page 102.

"There's been a lot of excitement while you were gone," Tom says. "It seems that Oliver was kidnapped two hours ago and that the *Alcor* is part of the ransom. Captain Hardy and O'Brien left port twenty minutes ago. They've been instructed to rendezvous with a ship operated by the kidnappers somewhere out at sea. We called the authorities, and that policeman over there came to investigate. He doesn't believe a word of our story."

"He thinks we're a bunch of kooks," Ari says.

"That's the bad news," Tom says. "The good news is that the captain left these envelopes for you, Leila, and Soto. We got ours too. They contain full pay for the cruise with additional airfare back to the States."

Leila is angry and upset. "Julius is definitely involved in the kidnapping," she says. "We can't let him get away with it."

"You're right," Soto says. "We owe it to Oliver."

You, Leila, and Soto go to the chief of police in Kingston. He gets a good laugh out of your story but refuses to help.

"We'll have to solve this mystery on our own," you say.

A short time later, Leila goes back to the States to get the federal authorities involved. You and Soto decide to spend the rest of the summer in Jamaica trying to find clues to Oliver's kidnapping.

Turn to page 97.

You and Oliver look out the side window of the plane. "There are lots of small islands down there," you say. "Maybe we can land in the ocean near one."

"Sure," Mike says, taking the helicopter down toward the surface. He glances over at you. "Reach behind you and grab that large orange bag," he says. "Then pull out the inflatable raft inside. It has its own carbon dioxide bottle attached. When we hit the water, open the valve on the bottle and toss the raft outside. Be sure to hold on to the tether, we don't want to lose the raft."

Mike approaches one of the islands. The helicopter skims along just above the surface for a few minutes before the motor cuts out completely. Then it plunges into the water. You toss out the raft and follow it into the sea.

The raft inflates automatically. You and Mike climb aboard, then help Oliver into the raft as the helicopter sinks below the waves. The water is crystal clear and not that deep. You watch the helicopter rotor as it spins, as if still in the air, all the way to the bottom.

You're relieved to see that you went down within half a mile of a small island. Mike removes a paddle attached to the inside of the raft and begins stroking toward shore. The current is with you, and you reach the island with surprising speed.

As the raft enters the surf, you, Mike, and Oliver jump out and pull it up on the beach.

Turn to page 46.

"I think we'd better go to the police," you say. You have barely gotten the words out when Julius rushes back up behind you. He has a wild expression on his face.

"I'm not sure I want to do that," he says. "I'll wait here while you go into town."

"Nonsense," Leila says. "You're coming along whether you want to or not."

"You'll regret this," Julius says under his breath.

Fortunately, you have no trouble finding a taxi. You, Soto, and Leila squeeze into the back, while Julius gets in the front.

"Take us to the police station," you say.

"The nearest one be in Kingston town," the driver says.

"All right," Leila says. "But hurry."

The taxi goes back up the country road. Up ahead is a crossroads. A sign indicates that a left turn will take you to Kingston—and the police station. Straight ahead will take you into the mountains, and clear across the island to Port Antonio on the north shore.

The driver slows down for the left turn. Suddenly Julius pulls out a gun! He turns halfway around so that he can cover the three of you in the backseat. "Straight ahead," he orders, pointing the gun at the driver.

"Anythin' you say, mon," the driver says. "Jus' don't be killin' me."

"Julius! What are you doing?" Leila shrieks. "Have you gone crazy?"

Turn to page 6.

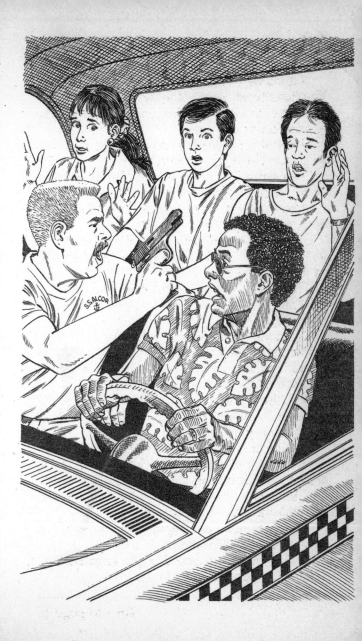

"That's right," the director says. "And of course you will be paid generously. But there may be danger involved also. I have to warn you about that."

"What kind of danger?" you ask.

"The children of very wealthy men are often targets for kidnappers," Ross says. "If there is such an attempt directed at Oliver, you may be right in the middle of it. Decide carefully if you want to take the job. You can tell me tomorrow."

That evening at dinner, you tell your family about the job offer from the director.

"It sounds too dangerous," your mother says.

"Look," you say, "there's danger in just crossing the street. I read somewhere that hundreds of people are killed every year slipping in the bathtub."

"Well then, you'll just have to make up your own mind about this," your mother says.

After dinner, you go up to your room to study. But you spend most of the night wondering whether to take the job the director has offered you. Cruising the Caribbean and teaching judo sounds exciting. But what about the danger Ross mentioned? Also, if you take the job, you'll miss out on the judo tournament and the lawn-cutting business.

*If you decide to take the job,
turn to page 61.*

*If you decide not to take the job,
turn to page 80.*

"I didn't hear anything, really," you say.

"We can't take a chance," Sean O'Brien, the first mate, says, looking you in the eye. "We'll have to dump you overboard."

"Now wait a minute, you can't—" you start to say, panic gripping you. But the captain knocks you out with a heavy, blunt object from behind before you have a chance to say any more.

The End

"You're not giving the kid to them," O'Brien growls. "Zorkin paid us to get rid of the runt and that's what we're gonna do."

O'Brien jumps aboard the lifeboat. Soto knocks him flat into the bow section with a high kick to the chest. At the same time, Tom reaches over from the raft and grabs Oliver. You get hold of Oliver as Tom pulls him out of the lifeboat and into the raft. The small craft overturns as you, Oliver, and Tom tumble into it. The three of you are dumped into the water.

You realize that Tom can't swim. In panic, he grabs you around the neck and pulls you under. You struggle to the surface with Tom still holding on. You can't see Oliver anywhere but you catch a momentary glimpse of O'Brien and Soto still fighting in the lifeboat. Then Tom pulls you under again.

When you manage to get back to the surface for the second time, you hear the sound of a helicopter over your head. You look up and see a rope dangling from its open door down to the surface of the water only a few feet away. Should you grab hold of it, you wonder, and pull yourself to safety? Or should you stay in the water until you find out if Oliver is all right?

If you grab hold of the rope,
turn to page 11.

If you stay in the water to look for Oliver,
turn to page 86.

A pretty, middle-aged woman with long, straight black hair is already seated in the back.

"My name is Leila," the woman says, holding out her hand for you to shake as the limo pulls away from the curb. "I'm Oliver's teacher—in most subjects. Of course, you'll be responsible for instructing him in judo. He needs all the self-defense skills he can get."

"Is he in some kind of danger?" you ask.

"Well, you can't be too careful in this day and age, can you?" the woman replies. "Particularly if you're the son of a billionaire."

"Am I also expected to be a bodyguard?" you ask.

"Not really," Leila says. "Oliver has a bodyguard named Julius. You'll meet him later."

The limousine speeds through the night. The rain patters on the roof. You peer out the tinted windows, but you can't see much, just blurred lights flashing by now and then.

Soon the limo arrives at a waterfront. It stops next to a long dock. The chauffeur opens the door, and you and Leila get out. A large, gleaming white yacht, illuminated by floodlights, is anchored at the end of the pier.

Turn to page 94.

"This is great!" Leila exclaims. "There should be a big celebration tonight."

"Can we get costumes too—like Halloween?" Oliver asks.

"I know from my last trip," Tom says, "that there's a costume shop on Victor Hugo Street, not far from here."

"Can we go there right now?" Oliver asks.

"The streets will be very crowded," Soto says. "But if we all stick together, we should be all right."

You, Oliver, Soto, Leila, and Julius go ashore and head for the costume shop, moving surprisingly easily among the revelers on the street. Inside the shop, Julius tries on a clown costume.

"That really seems to suit you," Leila says, laughing.

"So what," Julius grumbles.

You and Soto find Japanese samurai costumes but without the swords. Leila decides to be a Gypsy, and Oliver becomes a small pirate. Leila pays for the costumes, and you watch as they are put in boxes for your trip back to the yacht.

You spend the rest of the afternoon with the others putting on your costumes and getting ready for the night's festivities.

Turn to page 54.

"Do you think we can really find one?" Oliver asks. "Let's go."

"Hold on," Leila says. "I think someone from the ship should go with you two on this treasure hunt."

"I'll go with them," Julius says. "We won't go far. We'll meet you at the café over there in a while."

"All right, but make sure that you do," Leila says as she heads with you and Soto toward the café.

The three of you sit in front of the café. A waitress comes out and all of you order a lunch of hot, spicy chicken, called jerk, and fried bananas, called plantains.

As soon as she is finished eating, Leila stands up and scans the beach. "I don't see Oliver and Julius, or Robbie," she says.

"They're probably just out of sight up the beach," Soto says.

"I suppose so," Leila says with a sigh.

All of you order coffee. You sit there relaxing. However, Leila gets more and more anxious as time passes.

"They've been gone a long time," Leila says.

"Time can go by pretty fast when you're searching for treasure," Soto says.

"Wait here," you tell Leila. "Soto and I will check up the beach. We'll return in twenty minutes or so. And I'm sure Oliver and the others will be back before then."

Turn to page 64.

You dash forward to the companionway going up to the elevated platform where the bridge is located. The captain and the first mate are standing on the bridge, gazing at the sea ahead.

"Stop the ship! Oliver is overboard!" you holler.

"Overboard!" the captain exclaims. "I'll turn the ship around immediately."

The yacht runs a zigzag course, retracing its earlier path. But there's nothing to be seen except endless, glistening waves.

The next day, the *Alcor* continues to search. Everyone peers out across the sea, hoping to catch sight of Oliver.

By nightfall, the captain declares that it's no use.

No one says very much as the yacht heads back toward its home port on the southern coast of the United States. Leila has locked herself in her cabin and won't come out.

The next day, as you are walking past the yacht's small galley, Ari pulls you quickly inside. He has the water running full force out of the faucet in his sink to foil any eavesdropping.

"I was wandering around on deck the other evening just as the captain threw a beach towel over Oliver's head, then pushed him overboard. The first mate was with him," Ari whispers in your ear. "I've told Soto about it, but only you two. When we get to port, we'll go to the authorities."

Turn to page 119.

You stand at the rail with Oliver, Soto, Leila, and Julius as the *Alcor* eases alongside a pier on the waterfront. A rhythmic musical sound floats from the city.

"That's a strange kind of music," you say.

"It's reggae," Leila says. "You'll hear it everywhere in Kingston, and all of Jamaica, for that matter. The people who live here dance to it in the cafés, the restaurants, and even on the streets."

"Can we go ashore right away?" Oliver asks.

"Soon," Julius says. "I have a friend in town named Robbie. As soon as I find him, he'll show us around."

Julius jumps onto the pier from the yacht and heads for a group of storage buildings on the crowded docks. Soon he comes back accompanied by a tall dark-skinned man with a strange hairdo. His head is covered with long strands of tightly coiled hair hanging down to his shoulders. He's wearing a loose-fitting pink shirt and white jeans.

"This is my friend Robbie," Julius says as they come aboard the *Alcor*.

Turn to page 81.

You fall down on the beach, exhausted. As you rest, Mike tells you how the Eagle arranged for the submarine and helicopter to rescue Oliver from the *Alcor*. "Now I've got to finish the job and get us home safely," he says.

A few minutes later, Mike throws a small box down on the sand with disgust. "These things never work when you need them."

"You mean the automatic radio rescue beacon?" you ask.

"Right," Mike says.

"Do you know where we are?" Oliver asks.

"Yeah. This island is nowhere!" he replies.

The island is uninhabited, and there is no other land in sight. Fortunately you're able to find plenty of coconuts and wild berries to eat. They allow you to stay alive.

Six weeks later, you finally manage to signal a fishing boat with a bonfire you light on shore. The boat carries you to Miami, where Mike arranges for you and Oliver to fly home.

As you settle back into the comfortable airplane seat, you think how your summer vacation didn't work out the way you thought it would. But at least it was more interesting than mowing lawns.

The End

You, Oliver, Soto and Leila follow Julius and Robbie down to the end of the pier and climb aboard the minibus. The driver has a hairdo similar to Julius's, except that the braided strands are not as long.

"Where to?" the driver asks.

"First we'll go to the craft market," Julius says. "Then maybe—"

"But I want to see the pirates," Oliver interrupts. "Not some old stuffy market."

"There are no *real* pirates left. Only their ghosts—if there are such things," Leila says. "The market would be very interesting. You can see the things the people of the island produce and the kinds of foods they eat."

"No, no, no!" Oliver shouts.

"Can you help us out here?" Leila asks you. "Oliver seems to value your opinion."

Turn to page 106.

48

You decide to try to get off the ship as soon as you can. You have a hard time falling asleep, and when you do, you sleep fitfully.

You are startled awake in the morning by a loud knock at the door. You get up groggily and go over and open it—it's now unlocked. Leila, Oliver's tutor, is standing there.

"You've almost missed breakfast," she says. "I'll wait outside while you get dressed."

After you dress you follow Leila up the companionway toward the dining room. "I want to leave the ship as soon as I can," you tell her.

"You'll have to talk to the captain about that," Leila says. "He's still at breakfast, I believe."

When you reach the dining room, Leila walks directly over to the captain. "We have a problem here," she says. "Our new employee wishes to leave the ship."

"And why is that?" the captain asks, glaring at you.

"To start with, I was locked in my cabin all night," you say. "Suppose there had been a fire, or the ship started sinking. And also, I have reason to believe my cabin is bugged."

"I see," the captain says. "Unless you have proof of these charges, I don't know what I can do about them. However, we will be passing Great Exuma Island in the Bahamas in a few hours. I have no objection to stopping there briefly. If you wish to leave, you can."

Turn to page 8.

Two days later, back home, you go to the Martial Arts Center. You talk to Ross, the director, and explain as best you can about your Caribbean adventure.

"I'm still not sure what was going on," you tell him.

"It was a fiendish plot," Ross says. "Captain Hardy and his first mate were paid by Martin Zorkin to have Oliver 'accidentally' drown on the cruise. Zorkin was in dire financial straits and needed the money from Oliver's inheritance. In fact, Zorkin is now in jail in New York waiting to be tried for other crooked financial dealings. Julius knew nothing of the captain's plans and was plotting to kidnap Oliver and hold him for ransom himself. Soto, as you know, works for the Eagle, who was trying to protect Oliver. Leila knew nothing of either Captain Hardy's plans or Julius's. The submarine was sent by the Eagle to get Oliver to safety, but Hardy drove it away. Luckily, you and Soto were able to foil the plan."

"Lucky is right," you say. "That was some summer job."

"I'm sure it was," Ross says. "The important thing is that you did outstanding work. And what pleases me most is that you proved yourself a real master of judo."

The End

"I have a karate *gi* packed up in my cabin," Soto says. "I'll bring it next time."

"I'm ready," Oliver says. "What do I do first?"

"First you learn how to breathe," you say.

"Breathe? I know how to breathe," Oliver says.

"Proper breath control coordinated with the movement of your body is very important in the martial arts," Soto says.

"Exactly," you agree.

"Well, okay. If Soto feels that way, I'll breathe," Oliver says.

The three of you kneel on the deck. "Keep your back straight," you say, "and sit back gently on your heels. Relax your shoulders and let your arms hang loosely at your sides."

"How's this?" Oliver asks, shifting his body to the position you have described.

"Good," you say. "Now close your eyes and force all the air out of your lungs. Lean forward a bit as you do. When you have exhaled all you can, try to breathe out just a little more—and hold it."

Oliver follows your instructions.

"Now," you say, "breathe in very slowly, concentrating on your breath. Straighten up and you'll feel as if the air is filling up your whole body, not just your lungs. When you've breathed in as much air as you can, hold it for about ten seconds, then start over again."

Turn to page 82.

Ross leads you down the hall and into his office. He carefully closes the door after you are inside. Then he breaks into a smile and gestures for you to sit down.

"I hear that you're looking for a summer job," he says.

"I have been," you say. "Actually—"

You start to tell Ross about the idea that Chuck just came up with, but you don't get a chance to finish.

"I have a possibility for you," Ross says. "It's something I would love to do myself, if I weren't needed here at the center. But before I tell you any more about it, you must agree to keep whatever I say a secret, even if you decide not to take this on. Do I have your word?"

"Uh, sure," you say.

"Of course, you'll have to ask your parents—but discuss it with them only."

"I understand," you say.

"An anonymous donor, known only as the Eagle, is responsible for the creation of this center. A close friend of his, Martin Zorkin, has a young stepson named Oliver. Zorkin has asked us to recommend someone to instruct Oliver in the art of judo this summer."

Go on to the next page.

"That sounds great," you say.

"That's not all," the director continues. "You will do the teaching while on a cruise in the Caribbean aboard the *Alcor,* one of Zorkin's luxury yachts."

"The Caribbean Sea?" you ask.

Turn to page 36.

54

After a brief but beautiful scarlet and purple sunset, night settles on Fort-de-France. The drums get louder, and fireworks begin to light up the sky overhead.

"Remember, we all stick together," Leila says. "Don't get separated, especially you, Oliver."

"I'll keep an eye on him," Julius says. Oliver seems to wince.

You, Oliver, Soto, Julius, and Leila go ashore again to join the festivities. The captain and the crew have decided to spend the evening in one of the cafés on the waterfront.

The costumes of the crowd are brightly colored and filled with elaborate detail. Many kinds of wild animals are represented, including leopards, lions, and tigers.

The five of you follow along in the procession. Whole companies of drummers march between the towering papier-mâché structures of sea horses, dragons, and manta rays.

As you march, a figure dressed in a black costume with a glowing skeleton painted on it joins the parade next to you. Several others dressed as devils with bloodred costumes prance alongside, dancing to the music. You know this is all in good fun, but somehow you sense danger.

Turn to page 90.

On the way back to the café you ask Soto some questions, partly to keep your mind off Oliver and partly to find out more about this intriguing man.

"Your English is very good," you say. "Where did you learn it?"

"Mostly in high school," Soto says. "My grandparents were killed in the American invasion of Okinawa in the Second World War. My parents survived and became prosperous during the occupation. Also I was friends with many Americans as I grew up."

"How did you come to be working for Zorkin?" you ask.

"I came to the United States for college on a scholarship. After graduating, I applied to the Zorkin Corporation for a job."

"But after college, you got a job as a chauffeur and a deckhand?" you say.

Soto smiles slightly. "I know I can trust you," he says quietly. "I work secretly for the Eagle."

"I suspected that you were probably a spy of some sort," you say. "But I thought the Eagle and Zorkin were friends."

"You know the old saying, 'With friends like that, who needs enemies,' " he says.

Go on to the next page.

"I remember what Oliver said about Zorkin on the yacht," you say. "Do you really think he'd try to hurt his own stepson?"

"It's possible. There may be other things also," Soto says.

"Like what?" you ask.

"Kidnapping maybe, but that's what we have to find out," Soto says.

Turn to page 108.

You and Soto become friends as he helps you with Oliver's classes. You find out that his martial arts training is also very good. You're glad that he's aboard the ship, because most of the other crew members seem to want to keep to themselves.

Between lessons you spend hours watching the seabirds, the changing cloud formations, the waves, and the schools of dolphins that swim alongside the yacht.

Every once in a while you see a far-off streak in the water. It looks like the wake of a submarine periscope. That's impossible, you think. Still, you wonder if you should find out if the captain has noticed anything suspicious. Or maybe you should just keep watching the mysterious movement. You might be able to figure out what it is yourself.

If you decide to tell the captain about your strange sightings, turn to page 18.

If you decide to keep the sightings to yourself, turn to page 116.

60

You follow Soto up the gangplank to the deck, through a door, then down a ladder leading to the ship's interior. At the end of a long corridor, Soto stops. "Your cabin," he says, holding the door open for you. He follows you inside with your bags, putting them down next to a comfortable-looking bunk bed.

As Soto moves into the light, you notice his Oriental features. You wonder where he is from.

"I am from Okinawa. It's a Japanese island south of the main islands," he says, seemingly reading your mind. "Many great martial artists have come from there. You are skilled in judo?"

"I've been studying it for many years," you say. "I'm a black belt."

"A black belt already. Very good," he says. "You are going to teach Oliver?"

"That's what I'm supposed to do," you say.

Turn to page 66.

After school the next day, you go back to the Martial Arts Center and head straight for the director's office.

"I've decided to take the job," you tell Ross.

"Excellent," he says. "You are the best one for it. Sensei Yamamoto says that you are his top student."

"When do I start?" you ask.

Ross takes a thick folder out of one of his drawers and opens it on his desk. "Let's see," he says, riffling through the papers. "A taxi will pick you up on the evening of the fifteenth to take you to the airport. You will fly to Savannah, Georgia, where Zorkin's yacht is berthed. I understand that the last day of your school term is the tenth."

"Yes," you answer. "That should give me a chance to get things together before I leave."

"Then it's settled," the director says. "Good luck on the cruise, and remember, be careful and alert."

"I will," you say. "It sounds like a real vacation to me. I can hardly wait."

Turn to page 85.

Oliver doesn't look convinced. "I still want a gun," he mutters.

"*I'm* in charge of security on this yacht," Julius barks, "and you're not getting a gun."

"Why not?" Oliver says. "Suppose something happens to you? What if you fall overboard? Then what do I do?"

Before Julius can reply, Captain Hardy interrupts. "We have more important things to discuss right now," he says. "We must decide if our destination is going to be the island of Jamaica or the island of Martinique."

"I think you should pick the place," Leila tells Oliver. "After all, this cruise is part of your education."

"I don't know anything about either one of them," Oliver says.

"Let's see," Leila says. "Jamaica is a beautiful island with a fascinating history. Pirates used to plunder ships off its coast, and some of these old pirate haunts can still be explored today. Martinique is also very beautiful and has an exciting French and Caribbean culture. We may even be able to catch one of the island festivals there, with costumes, parades, and days of singing and dancing in the streets."

Go on to the next page.

"I still don't know which to pick. Which one would *you* choose?" Oliver asks you.

Pirates or a festival. It's a hard choice.

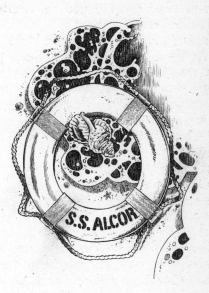

If you choose the island of Jamaica,
turn to page 112.

If you choose the island of Martinique,
turn to page 77.

64

You and Soto head down the wide beach. A few swimmers are snorkeling just offshore. Here and there, the ruins of brick buildings poke through the sand. You wonder if they are part of the old Port Royal itself, before it was destroyed.

The farther you walk, the more desolate the beach becomes. You pass what is left of an ancient fort. As you move around one of its crumbling corners, you are shocked to see five men clustered behind it. They look friendly enough— at first. Then, without warning, three of them block your path. The other two circle around behind you.

"Do you think we're in for trouble?" you ask Soto.

"One must always be ready for it," Soto says calmly.

"We're outnumbered," you say.

"In numbers, yes. But not in strength," Soto says.

You approach the three men in front of you.

Turn to page 9.

"I studied some tae kwon do and karate on my home island," Soto says. "If I'm not busy with my duties, maybe I can join your class."

"Sure," you say.

"If you need anything, press this," Soto says, pointing to a button in the center of the opposite wall. He opens an interior door revealing a lavatory hardly big enough to turn around in. Then he points to a spot on the ceiling. "Be careful," he says silently, using just his lips. "This cabin is bugged."

Soto closes the door behind him as he leaves. You unpack your things, then go over and try the door. It's locked! The only other exit in your cabin is a small round porthole. It doesn't look large enough for you to squeeze through. What is this all about? you wonder. The cabin is bugged and you are locked in!

You lie down on the bunk to decide whether you should stay on the ship or try to get off as soon as possible. There may be a logical explanation for your being locked in. On the other hand, you haven't even left shore and you are already beginning to feel trapped.

If you decide to stay on the ship, turn to page 91.

If you decide to get off as soon as you can, turn to page 48.

That evening, after retiring to your cabin, you open the porthole to enjoy the breeze. You're getting ready for bed when suddenly you hear a muffled cry. Something bright flashes by your porthole, followed by a splash. Your heart skips a beat as you look out and see Oliver thrashing about in the water.

You dash out of your cabin, down the corridor, and up a flight of stairs to the deck. You scream "Oliver is overboard" as you run to the stern and peer out across the moonlit water.

You quickly unfasten a life preserver from the railing. But Oliver is too far away to throw the life preserver to him.

You have a split second to decide whether to run up to the bridge and get the yacht to circle back or dive into the water with the life preserver.

*If you decide to dive in,
turn to page 99.*

*If you try to get the yacht to circle back,
turn to page 43.*

Jimmy gets up, a mean look on his face. He charges at you and grabs you around the neck. You purposely give him time to grab your sleeve with his other hand and pull you off balance. He sweeps you up with his right leg. You feel yourself lifted horizontally into the air, then dropped like a rock to the mat. This time Jimmy gets a round of applause. The judges award him ten points for his spectacular throw—enough for him to win the match.

You get up and walk off the mat, hoping that no one noticed that you purposely let down your guard for a moment.

In the match between Chuck and Jimmy, Chuck wins easily to become the champion. You are glad that he won and also glad that you didn't have to fight your best friend.

The End

70

"Let's try to find the pirates, or at least where they once hung out," you say.

"Great! Let's go!" Oliver exclaims.

The driver revs the minibus's engine and heads east from the docks, first through a section of town with many new buildings of white concrete, then through an older area teeming with life. You see men playing dominoes outside small, colorful houses. Children chase each other down the dusty streets. Soon, though, the city gives way to the countryside, covered with the lush vegetation of coconut palms, mango trees, and thick shrubbery.

Robbie instructs the driver to turn south onto a low tongue of land curving south, then west, away from the main part of the island. A half-hour later, you arrive at a small, sleepy-looking village at the end of the long, sandy peninsula. There are a few trees and houses as well as a tiny church.

All of you get out of the bus. Then the bus turns around and heads back toward Kingston.

"The bus will be back for us later," Julius says.

"This is where the pirates lived?" Oliver says, disappointed.

"It doesn't look like much now," Leila says, "but there once was a fabulous city here—the city of Port Royal. It was known as the wickedest city on earth, maybe the wickedest city that ever existed. It was the home of buccaneers, cutthroats, slavers—and Henry Morgan."

Turn to page 12.

That evening, you, Leila, Soto, and Oliver watch from the dock as the *Alcor* sails away.

"I have something for you and Leila," Soto says. "It's from the Eagle for your services."

"I'm not working for . . . who did you say?" Leila says.

"The Eagle," Soto says. "Let's just call him Oliver's protector." He hands you both an envelope. You find money inside. A lot of money!

"I can't take this much," Leila says. "I teach because I am dedicated to my work, not to how much money I can make."

"You deserve every penny," Oliver says. "You're the best teacher I ever had."

"Thank you, Oliver," Leila says.

"And you're the best judo instructor," Oliver tells you.

"I'm taking Leila and Oliver to another island where they will be safe," Soto tells you. "If you look closely, you'll see that there's also an airline ticket for you. A ticket home."

You find it really hard to say good-bye to Oliver, Soto, and Leila. You've all become good friends on this trip. You promise to keep in touch.

Turn to page 49.

"No problem," the constable says. "That big ship you see in the harbor is sailing for Miami in a few hours. I can easily arrange for you to be on it."

"Thank you, sir," you say.

"You can call me Thomas," the constable says.

"I don't have much money with me," you say.

"Don't worry about the money," Thomas says. "I have many friends that work on the cruise ship. They will take you as a favor to me."

You can hardly believe your luck. The cruise ship docks in Miami just after midnight. Fortunately, you have your birth certificate with you, and you get through immigration and customs around one a.m.

The bus station is within walking distance of the docks. You have just enough money for a ticket home. Your family is surprised to see you but glad to have you back.

Turn to page 80.

Julius's head collides with the side of the car, making a dull thud. You're glad that Oliver has remembered one of the basic moves of judo that you taught him.

Julius lets out another cry and tries to straighten up. That's all the time you need to kick the gun out of his hand. It discharges with a loud bang as it flies off to the side. A puff of dust rises as the bullet tears into the ground.

People in the nearby market scatter for cover. Seconds later, the police arrive. They arrest Julius on firearm charges. They also recognize and arrest Robbie, who is wanted for a number of crimes.

You, Soto, Oliver, and Leila take the minibus back to the yacht.

"We exposed one criminal among us," Soto says on the way. "But I wonder if Julius has an accomplice in the crew."

"I think we still have to be careful, just in case," you say.

Captain Hardy seems very surprised when you tell him what happened. Or is he just feigning surprise? you wonder.

Early the next morning, the captain starts the engines and orders all lines cast off from the dock. You and Leila race up to the bridge.

"Can we just leave like this, Captain?" Leila asks. "Don't we have to testify in court about Julius?"

Turn to page 26.

"I think we should go to the market first," you say.

"Oh, all right," Oliver says. "But I don't want to stay there long."

"You won't," Julius says.

The minibus drives through the city to the craft market, a sprawling collection of open sheds and stalls. Hundreds of merchants are hawking their wares—wood carvings, straw baskets, straw hats, costume jewelry, and island T-shirts. One area even has import items like radios and television sets.

Oliver seems most interested in the wood carvings. He talks Leila into buying him a two-foot-high African figure holding a spear. She explains that the figurine is a maroon—one of a fierce group of early slaves in Jamaica who refused to be controlled by English rule. Oliver carries it with him as he pushes his way through the crowds of tourists surrounding the stalls.

Turn to page 115.

Early the next morning, a large island appears on the horizon. As you get closer, you see majestic blue mountains rising up from the sea. A long line of sparkling white beach separates the sea from the land. You have reached Jamaica.

Soon Kingston, the capital of the island, and its waterfront stretches ahead. Large high-rise hotels gleam white in the morning sun. Behind the city, the mountains rise steeply to a wreath of clouds at their summit.

Turn to page 45.

"I pick Martinique," you say.

"Martinique it is!" the captain exclaims. "We'll take the Mona Passage down between Hispaniola and Puerto Rico. Then we'll follow the line of islands that make up the West Indies to Martinique."

"Christopher Columbus discovered and explored these islands in the years following 1492. He named them the Indies because he thought they were close to India," Leila says.

"Every one of them is a beauty," Tom, the ship's engineer, says. "St. Croix, Montserrat, Guadeloupe, Dominica, St. Lucia, Grenada. There are many others."

"After the Spanish colonized them in the fifteen-hundreds," Leila goes on, "most of the original inhabitants, the Carib Indians, died of diseases brought there by the Europeans. The Spanish then transported large numbers of slaves from Africa to work on their sugar and tobacco plantations. Eventually, pirates and privateers attacking their ships weakened the Spanish power. The other European nations, mainly England and France, then moved in and seized some of the islands. Many, like Jamaica, are now independent countries, though Martinique is still French."

"This is quite a history lesson," you say.

Leila grins at you. "I can't help it," she says. "I told you I'm a teacher."

Turn to page 23.

You push your way straight through the crowd, leaving Soto behind. The dancers and revelers swirl around you as you try to catch sight of Oliver. You don't notice one of the large floats bearing down on you.

You feel a sharp pain in your leg as the float knocks you to the ground. Several of the dancers stop to help.

"*Mon Dieu!*" one of them exclaims. "I think you have broken ze leg."

An ambulance parked nearby in case of any festival casualties pulls up. The medics lift you inside.

At the hospital, the doctors set the fracture, and put your leg in a cast. You're up and around on crutches in a few hours.

When you get out of the hospital the next day, the festival is over. And the *Alcor* has left port! No one at the waterfront or customs can give you any information about where it was headed or who was aboard.

Fortunately, a local dojo takes you in. You become an assistant teacher of judo. You don't have to know French to demonstrate *wazas* and *katas*.

At the end of the summer, you manage to sign on to a freighter as a deckhand for the trip back home.

You never do find out what happened to Oliver or the others. You just hope that they're all right.

The End

The next day you go to see Ross at the Martial Arts Center. You tell him of your decision.

"You have a right to make your own choices," Ross says. "The trip on the *Alcor* is just not for you."

"You're not angry?" you ask.

"Certainly not. Actually, I'm glad you'll be here for this summer's annual judo tournament. It will be more interesting with you participating."

You leave Ross's office feeling a lot better. You run into Chuck in the hall.

"Do you still want to be my partner in the lawn-cutting business?" he asks.

"Sure," you say.

"And are you going to enter the judo tournament?"

"Yes," you say.

"What if we have to fight each other?" Chuck says. "We're best friends and business partners."

"That's true," you say. "Let's cross that bridge when we come to it."

The lawn-cutting business turns out to be brisk. You have as many lawns to cut during the day as you can handle. Fortunately, the judo tournament is held at night.

Rows of chairs are set up around the main hall of the dojo. Mostly it is the friends and families of the contestants who have come to see the tournament. You can feel the excitement in the air.

Turn to page 100.

You wonder how Julius found Robbie so fast but, after a second glance, figure that he would be hard to miss.

Robbie notices both you and Oliver looking openmouthed at his hair.

"I see you inspectin' me dreads," Robbie says. "They show that I am Rasta."

"Robbie is a Rastafarian," Julius explains. "That means that he belongs to a very popular religion here in Jamaica."

"I'm sorry, I didn't mean to stare," you say.

"Robbie is proud of his dreadlocks, as they call them," Julius says. "I'm sure he doesn't mind. Anyway, Robbie has a rented minibus waiting at the end of the pier."

Turn to page 47.

82

When Oliver has gone through the cycle several times, you tell him to stop and let his body relax completely.

"This is great," Oliver says. "I feel like I'm floating."

Soto has been doing the exercise along with Oliver. "Now you are ready to learn more about the art of judo," he says.

"When do I learn how to give a chop to the side of somebody's head?" Oliver says.

"Judo is a method of defending yourself, not attacking," you say. "One of the best techniques of defense is to run away."

"Run away?" Oliver repeats. "What if I can't get away?"

"Very simple," you say. "You disarm your attacker, or divert his or her attack away from you and escape. *Ju* means gentle and *do* means way. *Judo* is the 'gentle way.' "

"Gentle? I don't want to be gentle," Oliver says.

Go on to the next page.

"Judo is not always gentle," Soto says. "Jujitsu, the original form of judo, was created by the Samurai warriors of ancient Japan. They were famous for their skills as swordsmen, but if disarmed on the battlefield, they used their jujitsu skills in hand-to-hand combat. I learned about them in school on Okinawa."

"Soto is right," you say. "Gentle may not be the right word. Judo movements should be flowing—like water. Water yields and flows around obstacles, yet it can wear down the hardest stone."

Turn to page 7.

The evening of your departure, a taxi pulls up in front of your house. You carry your bags over to it and wave good-bye to your parents and little sister as you get in. Then the taxi heads into the night.

Twenty minutes later, you arrive at the airport. You spot a sleek, twin-engine executive jet parked on the far side of a runway. A uniformed guard opens the door of the taxi and helps you transfer your things to the plane.

As soon as you are inside, the door closes and the plane begins taxiing down the runway. When you are airborne, the copilot comes back to the passenger cabin to see if you are all right.

"We'll land in Savannah in a few hours," he says. "If you'd like to get some rest, these seats fold all the way back."

You decide to do just that, leaning back in one of the comfortable chairs. Soon the hum of the motors lulls you to sleep.

Sometime later, the copilot gently shakes you awake. It's quiet except for what sounds like rain outside. You realize that the plane has landed. You get up groggily and follow the copilot to the now-open door of the plane. A limousine is parked a short distance away. The chauffeur comes over with an umbrella. He shields you from the rain on your way to the limo and puts your bags in the trunk as you get in.

Turn to page 39.

You can't leave Oliver behind to drown. Using what is left of your strength, you maneuver around and see Oliver thrashing about in the water not far away. You swim over to him and wrap your left arm around his waist.

"Just relax, Oliver. We'll be all right!" you shout.

With your right arm, you start to stroke toward the lifeboat. It's drifted several yards away. Suddenly someone grabs hold of your foot under the water. You realize that it must be Tom again. He starts trying to use your leg to climb back to the surface. You let go of Oliver for a moment so that you can shake Tom free. But Oliver, screaming in fear, clings to you.

The weight is too much. You sink below the water with both of them pulling you down. As darkness surrounds you, you realize that this time you're not going to make it back to the surface.

The End

At the same moment, Leila arrives with two policemen. Oliver follows behind them. Despite your pleas, they take all of you to the station and lock you up for the night.

The next day you are brought before the magistrate.

"It was all a prank," the captain explains, trying hard to look innocent.

"Yes, that's right," Julius says. "We were just having a little fun."

"I can understand that," the magistrate says in a thick French accent. "But I expect you, Captain Hardy—and your yacht—to have left Martinique by sundown, *s'il vous plaît.*"

Turn to page 71.

88

"I'll go with you, Oliver," you say.

"Thanks," Oliver tells you. "You're a real friend."

A lifeboat is lowered from the *Alcor,* and Tom and Soto row you and Oliver out to the submarine.

"I don't think they intend to harm Oliver—or you," Soto says.

"I hope you're right," you say.

The boat pulls alongside the sub, and you and Oliver climb aboard.

"Good luck," Soto says as the lifeboat backs away.

The men on deck hurry you and Oliver through a hatch and down into the submarine.

"Prepare to submerge!" you hear a crewman order.

The hatches clang shut above you. Horns sound throughout the ship. One of the sailors leads you and Oliver to a small compartment.

"The captain will see you as soon as we're underway," he says.

The submarine tilts forward, submerging. After a few minutes, it levels out—you have no idea at what depth. A uniformed officer comes into your compartment. "I'm Captain Banon," he says. "I've been sent by the Eagle to get you to safety."

"The Eagle? My stepfather's friend?" Oliver asks.

Turn to page 28.

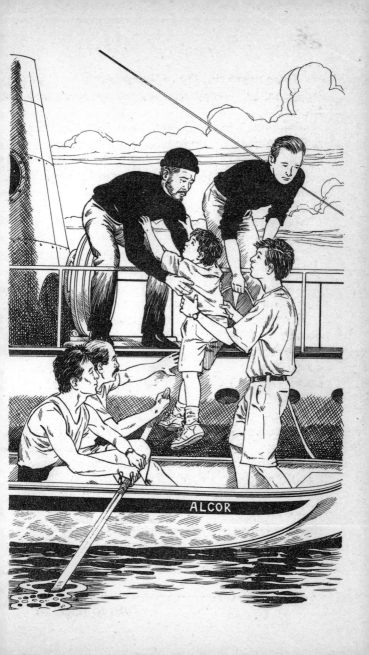

Your instincts are all too accurate. Without warning, the skeleton grabs Oliver and, swinging him over his shoulder, carries him off into the crowd. You and Soto start after him, but the devil figures block your way.

After a short scuffle, you and Soto are able to push the devils aside. But the skeleton is already entering an alley up ahead on the far side of the crowd.

The street in front of you is packed, and the skeleton is getting away. You must decide the best way to chase him. Should you push directly through the crowd, or race around it?

If you push straight through the crowd, turn to page 78.

If you race around it, turn to page 30.

Even though the *Alcor* and its crew have you worried, you decide to give the cruise a try. You calm your nerves and settle down to sleep.

When you wake up the next morning, the yacht is rocking gently, and you can feel the faint vibration of the engines rumbling below. You bend over near the porthole and peer out. There is nothing but ocean as far as you can see. You get dressed, then go over and try the cabin door. It's unlocked. You open it cautiously and peek out into the corridor. No one is there.

You leave your cabin and walk down the quiet hall toward the stairway at the other end. Suddenly, out of nowhere, a heavyset man with a blond crew cut blocks your way.

"Ah, you must be our judo expert," the man says in a deep voice.

"I'm looking for Leila . . . or Soto," you stammer.

"Of course," he says, reaching out with a large hand to shake yours. "I'm Julius. I'm responsible for security on this yacht."

"You're Oliver's bodyguard?" you ask.

"Bodyguard?" Julius chuckles. "Leila probably told you that. Well, I may be that—among other things. Oliver will also have to learn to look out for himself. With your help, eh?"

"I hope so," you say.

"Well, come along," Julius says. "Everyone's in the dining room."

Turn to page 14.

"My real father's will left me millions of dollars in a trust fund," Oliver says. "If anything happens to me, my stepfather will get it."

"But your stepfather is already a billionaire. Why would he want your money?" you say.

"They say he's a billionaire," Soto says. "But nobody knows what his real financial situation is."

Oliver nods. "I've only seen my stepfather a couple of times. I've been in private boarding schools since my real father died," he says. "This cruise is the first time I've been anyplace else since then."

"That's awful," you say. "Can't you—"

The hulking figure of Julius appears in the doorway. "It's time for Oliver's morning lesson with Leila," he says.

"Oh, darn," Oliver says. "She's probably going to make me study math again. Can we have a judo lesson later?"

"We will, definitely," you say. "Sometime this afternoon."

"I kind of like Oliver," you tell Soto, after the boy has left for his lesson. "But I'm not sure I believe this thing about his stepfather."

Go on to the next page.

"What Oliver says may be true," Soto says. "Or it may just be a childhood fantasy caused by fears from his real father's death. I'm trying to keep an eye on things in any event."

"I will too," you say.

"Now I must go and clean the cabins," Soto says. "That's my job on this cruise. We will talk later."

Turn to page 117.

"There she is," Leila says. "The *Alcor*. Ninety feet long and twenty feet wide. The *Alcor* is diesel propelled, but she has all the speed and power of a racing yacht."

A tall, bearded man in a black turtleneck sweater and a white naval cap is standing at the foot of a gangplank leading up to the deck of the yacht. He has a patch over one eye.

"This is Captain Hardy," Leila says, introducing you.

"Welcome aboard," he says in a gruff voice. You're not sure he means it.

The chauffeur behind you picks up your bags. "Soto will show you to your cabin," Leila says. "You will meet the rest of the crew and Oliver in the morning."

Turn to page 60.

Soto deftly trips the other man. He goes sprawling on the sand. The remaining two men run off.

"They may be going to get others," you say.

"I don't think so," Soto says. "If they do, we can take care of them."

"I didn't know you were so good at self-defense," you say. "Why didn't Zorkin get you to teach Oliver?"

Soto laughs. "I have enough trouble just doing my regular job on the yacht," he says.

The man that Soto tripped is still lying on the sand, holding his ankle. You reach down and help him to his feet.

"We're looking for a young boy. He's with a tall, heavyset man and a Rasta," Soto tells him.

"Oh, lawd. You try to kill me, then be askin' about a Rasta and young boy?" the man says.

"It was a fair fight, I'd say," Soto says.

"You are right about that, mon," the man says. "No, I haven't seen the ones you be lookin' for. They not be comin' on this beach."

"How is your ankle?" you ask.

"I be walkin' all right," the man says.

"Then get away from here and stay out of trouble," Soto says as the man limps off.

"We've gone far enough up the beach," you say. "We'd better start back. Leila will be worried about us too."

Turn to page 56.

But no clues turn up.

Finally, at the end of the summer, Soto flies home to see his family in Okinawa, and you fly home yourself. After saying hello to your family, you rush to the Martial Arts Center. Ross, the director, is anxious to see you.

"I talked to the Eagle on the phone and he brought me up-to-date on the *Alcor* ordeal," he says. "The kidnappers, including Julius and Robbie, escaped with the ransom as well as the ship, which has disappeared. However, I understand that the authorities are hot on its trail. As it turns out, they weren't working for Zorkin at all. They were just after the money."

"What happened to Oliver and Leila?" you ask with concern.

"According to the Eagle, Oliver is safe with his mother. He was released once the ransom was delivered. Leila now has an important position in the Eagle's organization," Ross adds. "Oh, and speaking of that, how would you like to work directly for the Eagle? He could really use a judo master like you on his staff."

Memories of all the excitement and danger of your summer cruise come rushing back to you. "That's something I'd really like to think about," you say.

The End

You kick off your shoes, sling the life preserver over your shoulder, and dive into the dark water. You don't realize that the *Alcor* is speeding away from you as you swim toward where you last saw Oliver. When you reach the spot, there is no one there.

You look back and see the lights of the yacht, already a great distance away, pinpoints on the horizon. You float there, hoping the lights will start coming back in your direction—but they don't.

You hang on to the life preserver, wondering how long it will be before the *Alcor* comes back looking for you. It never does.

Another ship may spot you—if the sharks don't find you first.

The End

100

There are thirty-two contestants, which means that thirty-one individual matches have to be held on the three nights of the tournament. Each match lasts five to ten minutes. Points are scored by two judges for throws, pin-downs, and arm locks as well as for overall skill.

Both you and Chuck have a fairly easy time in your preliminary matches. For you, the toughest opponents are the "lurkers" who hold back waiting for you to attack so that they can counterthrow. You are almost beaten and eliminated from the contest when one of your opponents grabs your collar and pulls your head all the way back. Fortunately you manage to reach down and grab his legs, toppling him to the mat.

You also watch Chuck's matches. You realize how good he is. If you have to fight him, he's going to be a tough opponent. But then you're not sure you *want* to fight him—it would be hard to put all your effort into beating your best friend.

By the third night, you have both reached the semifinal round. It's obvious that you and Chuck will end up as the final contenders. You have a hard time deciding what to do.

If you decide to fight Chuck, turn to page 22.

If you try to find a way to get out of fighting him, turn to page 29.

You decide to concentrate on preparing Oliver's lesson.

At noon, everyone aboard, except the first mate that you still haven't met, reassembles for lunch. Oliver looks glum after his morning class with Leila. The others seem lost in their own thoughts.

"Where should I give Oliver his judo lesson?" you ask Leila.

"At the stern," she says. "There's an open deck there. I'll have Ari move the lounge chairs out of the way."

"I hope this will be fun," Oliver says.

"The main purpose of my instruction is to help you learn self-defense," you say. "But if you do as I say, and try hard, I'm sure you will have fun too."

"Okay," Oliver says. "I can do that."

After lunch, you, Oliver, and Soto go back near the stern of the yacht. There is a surprisingly large open space there. Ari is folding up the last of the deck chairs and taking them off to the side. He has also laid down a mat for you.

You open a satchel you've brought along and take out your *gi* and a smaller one for Oliver. "I have a *judogi* for you," you say as you hand it to him. "I hope it fits." Oliver puts his on while you do the same.

"Hey, this is really cool," Oliver says.

Turn to page 51.

"It's Captain Hardy!" Soto exclaims.

"That's right," Hardy says. "I'm the captain, and you are still under my command. You'd better do what I tell you."

"Forget it," Soto says. "We're taking you to the police."

"I don't think you'll be doing that," a voice says from the shadows. You look over and see O'Brien, the first mate, in his devil costume. His mask is now off. He has a gun pointed at you and Soto. "I'm taking you back to the yacht and locking you up in the brig for insubordination."

"You won't get me," Oliver says as he takes off down the street.

"Come back here, you little—" O'Brien starts. But his attention is distracted for a moment. Soto moves so fast that his leg is a blur. His flying kick knocks the gun from O'Brien's hand.

Turn to page 87.

"Robbie may have taken Oliver to see some of the sights of Kingston," Julius says. "He may even have taken Oliver back to the *Alcor*."

"I see it now," Leila shouts at Julius. "You're part of this whole thing. Well, you're not going to get away with it. I'm going to—"

Leila charges Julius with a clenched fist. Julius, of course, is twice her size, but he backs off, startled. "I'm not going to put up with these accusations," he says. Then he turns and stomps off, disappearing behind the café.

Leila slumps down in a chair and covers her face with her hands.

"What do we do now?" Soto asks.

"I think we either go to the police or go back to the *Alcor* and alert Captain Hardy to what has happened," you say.

"Julius might be right about the police," Soto says.

"I know," you say. "But we may be wasting precious time going back to the ship."

If you decide to go to the police, turn to page 34.

If you decide to go back to the Alcor, *turn to page 111.*

"You take Robbie," Soto says. "I'll take Julius."

Robbie lets go of Oliver and lunges at you. You grab his sleeve with both hands and toss him over your shoulder in a classic judo throw. He lands with a thud on the hard pavement.

"Ow!" he cries out. "You broke me back!"

You turn in time to see Soto stop a punch from Julius with his open hand. Soto brings his other hand down on Julius's wrist with a karate chop. You remember that Soto is trained in several of the martial arts.

You hear a snap as Julius's wrist shatters.

"Yow!" Julius cries out. "I'll kill you." He pulls a gun out with his uninjured hand.

At the same moment, Leila appears from the market. "What's going on?" she exclaims. "Oliver, are you all right?"

Oliver has climbed out of the car trunk. "Julius and that other guy were trying to kidnap me," he yells.

"So, Julius, you are finally exposed for what you really are—a rat," Leila shouts.

"You'd better back off while I get into this car, or I'll blow somebody's head off," Julius says, waving his gun in your direction.

Julius takes a few steps toward Oliver, who has bent over to pick up his carving. He reaches down and tries to seize the boy. But with one swift motion, Oliver grabs him by the collar and pulls him forward.

Turn to page 74.

106

You are on the spot. Oliver watches you expectantly. You'd like to make him happy and wouldn't mind exploring the pirate haunts yourself. Then you notice Julius glaring at you impatiently. Maybe you *should* go to the craft market as he suggested.

"If I make the decision, will everybody go along with it?" you ask.

After some arguing, they all agree.

*If you decide to explore old pirate haunts,
turn to page 70.*

*If you decide to go to the craft market first,
turn to page 75.*

Just then, Oliver comes out on deck with Leila. "This is monstrous," Leila says. "They can't do this."

"I'm afraid they can," Captain Hardy says. "Otherwise they'll blow us out of the water."

The crew hurriedly tries to come up with a plan. Then Oliver speaks up. "I'll go. But will you go with me?" he asks you.

"Me?" you say.

"I don't want to go alone," Oliver says.

It might be dangerous going with Oliver, you realize. You have no idea who is on the sub or what they are up to. On the other hand, it might be just as dangerous not to go. You don't know if the people on the submarine will keep their word not to sink the *Alcor*.

*If you decide to go with Oliver,
turn to page 88.*

*If you decide not to go with Oliver,
turn to page 20.*

"We?" you say.

"You've been working for the Eagle without realizing it," Soto says.

You are stunned by Soto's remarks. But now that you know you are involved in this dangerous scheme, you want to find out more. "Okay," you say, "why would the Eagle be concerned about Oliver?"

"Oliver's real father was also a friend of the Eagle's, perhaps a truer friend," Soto says. "And now the Eagle is depending on us to keep Oliver safe."

When you get back to the café, Leila and Julius are arguing heatedly. Oliver and Robbie are not there.

"I've known Robbie for years and I just don't believe he's a kidnapper," Julius is telling Leila.

"You'll see when the ransom note comes," Leila says.

"What happened?" you ask.

"When we got to the spot where Robbie said we might find a Spanish coin," Julius says, "a car suddenly roared up. Robbie grabbed Oliver and forced him inside, then jumped in after him. The car sped away before I could do anything. It all happened so fast."

Go on to the next page.

"I think we should go right to the police," Leila says.

"Getting involved with the police here can be a sticky situation," Julius says. "I don't think we know all the facts. This may just be a misunderstanding."

"A misunderstanding!" Leila exclaims. "Are you crazy?"

Turn to page 103.

You, Soto, and Leila manage to find a taxi to take you back to the *Alcor.* Julius has not returned. After a half-hour trip back to Kingston and a ten-minute drive through the twisting streets of the city, you arrive at the docks. Up ahead is the *Alcor*'s pier. A police car is parked at the foot of the pier and a small crowd is standing around a policeman.

"Looks like there might be trouble over there," the cabdriver says.

"That's not all," you say. "The *Alcor* is gone."

You, Soto, and Leila jump from the cab and, avoiding the group surrounding the policeman, run toward the pier.

"This *is* the right pier, isn't it?" you say.

"The ship must have moved to a new berth. Maybe the policeman knows," Soto says.

You go over and ask him.

"The officer looks up from his notebook. "You three from the *Alcor?*"

"That's right, we—" you start.

"You'd better talk to those two men over there," he says, pointing toward the now-empty berth.

You see Tom, the yacht's engineer, and Ari, the chef, standing together a short distance away.

You hurry over to them. "Is anything wrong?" you ask.

Turn to page 32.

"I think I'd pick Jamaica," you say.

"Then we'll go there," Oliver says.

"Very good," the captain says. "Then I'll be on my way to the bridge. We'll set a course down through the Bahamas, and then through the Windward Channel between Cuba and Haiti."

After the captain leaves, Ari serves the remaining coffee and pastries. Leila, Tom, and Julius finish eating, then go off to prepare for their morning duties. That leaves you, Oliver, and Soto alone at the table.

"I think it would be better if we decided from the beginning to be friends," you say to Oliver. "I'll do my best to teach you the things that I know about self-defense."

Oliver gives you a long look. "All right. I guess I have to trust somebody. Actually I trust Soto, but no one else on this ship. Especially Julius and the captain."

"You don't trust the captain?" you say.

"Did you know that he has all the cabins bugged, so he can spy on everybody?" Oliver says. "He's also planning this scheme with my stepfather. They want to get me killed. It's supposed to look like an accident."

Go on to the next page.

"Isn't Julius protecting you?" you say.

"Sure. If you believe that, you'll believe anything," Oliver says.

"Do you really think your stepfather wants to get you killed?" you say. "Why would he want to do that?"

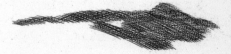

Turn to page 92.

You get interested in the straw hats and try a few on. Suddenly you realize that you've lost track of Oliver. You run outside and look around for him frantically.

Soto is right behind you. "Don't worry," he says. "I'm sure he's with Leila—or Julius."

"It's his being with Julius that I'm worried about," you say.

"Why? Is there something—" Soto's voice is interrupted by a shriek. It sounds as if it is coming from several sheds away.

"This way, quick!" you tell Soto.

You weave through the crowd and round a corner in time to see Julius and Robbie shoving Oliver into the trunk of a car. His carving lies on the ground beside it.

Turn to page 104.

116

You decide not to alert the captain—yet.

From time to time, you look out at the ocean, trying to spot the periscope, or whatever it is. You don't see it again and begin to wonder if you just imagined it.

One morning, as you are getting up, you hear a tremendous explosion near the ship. You race over and look out the porthole. A submarine has surfaced only fifty yards from the yacht! You see a flash from a cannon mounted on its foredeck. Several seconds later, another explosion rocks the yacht. A column of water rises about twenty yards in front of the *Alcor*. The sub seems to be firing warning shots.

You get dressed as fast as you can and run up on deck.

Julius is the first person you see. "What's going on?" you ask.

"A high seas holdup!" he says, shaking his fist in the direction of the sub. "They intend to sink us if we don't hand over Oliver."

"That's terrible!" you say. "Isn't there anything we can do?"

"We have armament, but it's still covered up on deck," Julius says. "If only we'd had some warning."

A man sporting a short graying beard and dressed in a black turtleneck shirt is standing on the deck of the submarine with a megaphone. "The boy will not be harmed. We are removing him from your custody for his own protection. You have five minutes to comply."

Turn to page 107.

Soto goes off on his errands, and you step out on deck. The ocean stretches in all directions. Chattering sea gulls fly around the yacht, which rolls gently as it plows through the water. Something bothers you about the crew and this whole cruise—but you can't put your finger on it. If Oliver is right about his stepfather, you wonder, why did Zorkin recruit you to come on this trip and teach Oliver self-defense? To prove later that he did everything he could to protect his stepson? Or does he have another plan in which you could be in as much danger as Oliver!

You certainly have a lot of questions. If you look around the ship, you might find some answers. On the other hand, it might be better to keep a low profile for now and see what you can find out just by doing your job and keeping an eye on things.

If you decide to look around the ship, turn to page 25.

If you decide to lay low and prepare for Oliver's first judo lesson, turn to page 101.

Two days later, when the *Alcor* docks, the police are waiting on the pier. But instead of arresting the captain, they take you, Soto, and Ari into custody. The captain and the first mate claim they saw the three of you toss Oliver overboard.

"What'll we do?" you ask as the police hustle you, Soto, and Ari toward the police station, locked in the back of a patrol car. "It's their word against ours."

"Don't worry," Soto says, taking something out from the inside pocket of his jacket. "I found these tapes in Captain Hardy's stateroom while I was cleaning it. He must have forgotten to lock them in the ship's safe. I played a couple of them. They're tapes he made bugging the various rooms on the yacht. He even recorded his own conversations with the first mate about their evil plans to hurt Oliver."

"That wasn't too smart of him," Ari says.

"Who knows why people do things?" you say. "But the tapes will break this case wide open and send Captain Hardy and O'Brien to prison where they belong."

The End

ABOUT THE AUTHOR

RICHARD BRIGHTFIELD is a graduate of Johns Hopkins University, where he studied biology, psychology, and archaeology. For many years he worked as a graphic designer at Columbia University. He has written many books in the Choose Your Own Adventure series, including *Hurricane!*, *Master of Kung Fu*, *Hijacked!*, *Master of Tae Kwon Do*, *Master of Karate*, and *Master of Martial Arts*. In addition, Mr. Brightfield has coauthored more than a dozen game books with his wife, Glory. The Brightfields and their daughter, Savitri, live in southern Florida.

ABOUT THE ILLUSTRATOR

FRANK BOLLE studied at Pratt Institute. He has worked as an illustrator for many national magazines and now creates and draws cartoons for magazines as well. He has also worked in advertising and children's educational materials and has drawn strips, including *Annie* and *Winnie Winkle*. He has illustrated many books in the Choose Your Own Adventure series, including *Master of Kung Fu*, *Return of the Ninja*, *You Are a Genius*, *Through the Black Hole*, *The Worst Day of Your Life*, *Master of Tae Kwon Do*, *The Cobra Connection*, *Hijacked!*, *Master of Karate*, *Invaders from Within*, *The Lost Ninja*, *Daredevil Park*, *Kidnapped!*, and *Master of Martial Arts*. A native of Brooklyn Heights, New York, Mr. Bolle now lives and works in Westport, Connecticut.